DON'T *Blame Me*

By Eleanor Robins

CARTER HIGH
CHRONICLES

Back-up Quarterback
The Best Week Ever
Boy of Their Dreams
Don't Blame Me
The Easy Way
The Fastest Runner
It Is Not a Date
One Date Too Many
The Right Kind of Win
Too Late

ISBN-13: 978-1-61651-306-1
ISBN-10: 1-61651-306-3
eBook: 978-1-60291-954-9

Printed in Guangzhou, China
0910/09-42-10

15 14 13 12 11   1 2 3 4 5

Chapter 1

June was in science class. It was her last class of the day. It was almost time for class to start. Mrs. Frey was her teacher.

June sat next to Rose. Rose was her best friend. They were both on the volleyball team.

"I wish Zack was in this class," June said.

Zack was her boyfriend.

Rose said, "Why? Because you like him so much?"

"I do like him a lot. But that isn't why. He called last night. He needed help on science. His teacher isn't doing what we are doing. So I couldn't help him," June said.

Rose said, "Too bad. I hope he can find someone to help him."

The bell rang.

Mrs. Frey started class. Mrs. Frey said, "Get out your homework. We will go over it first."

June and Rose quickly got out their homework.

"Gail, you tell us the first answer," Mrs. Frey said.

Gail sat on the other side of the room. She started to give her answer. But she was very quiet. It was hard to hear her.

"Can you hear her? I can't," Rose said to June.

Mrs. Frey said, "June, stop talking. Class has started."

That made June mad. She was not talking.

June said loudly, “I was not talking. So don’t blame me for something I didn’t do.”

Rose quickly said, “Sorry, Mrs. Frey. I was the one talking. Not June.”

“So you were wrong. It wasn’t me,” June said.

Mrs. Frey said, “See me after class, June.”

“Why? I didn’t do anything,” June said.

“Be quiet, June. Just stay,” Rose said. But she said it so only June could hear her.

June didn’t say any more. But she was mad. Why should she have to stay? She had not done anything wrong. She was not the one who was talking.

June was glad when class was over. She was ready to get out of that class. But first she had to find out what Mrs. Frey wanted.

She walked over to Mrs. Frey's desk. Rose walked over there too.

The rest of the class hurried out of the room.

Rose said, "Did you want to see me too, Mrs. Frey? I was the one talking. Not June."

"No, Rose. Only June," Mrs. Frey said.

Rose looked at June. She said, "I'll wait for you in the hall, June."

Rose hurried out into the hall.

June said, "Why do you want to talk to me? Rose told you she was the one talking. Not me."

Mrs. Frey said, "It is not about who was talking. I am worried about you, June."

That surprised June.

"Why are you worried about me? There isn't anything wrong with me," June said.

"You are quick to lose your temper, June. Don't let your temper get the best of you. It hurts you when you do," Mrs. Frey said.

June didn't let her temper get the best of her. So she didn't know why Mrs. Frey said that.

"Is that all you wanted to see me about?" June asked.

"Yes," Mrs. Frey said.

June said, "Can I go now? I have volleyball practice."

Mrs. Frey said, "Yes, June. But think about what I said."

Why? What Mrs. Frey said about her quick temper was not true.

June hurried out of the class. She could hardly wait to go to volleyball practice.

Chapter 2

Rose was waiting for June in the hall.

"Does Mrs. Frey still think you were talking?" Rose asked.

June said, "That wasn't what she wanted. She said she was worried about me."

Rose looked surprised. She said, "Why?"

"She thinks I let my temper get the best of me. I don't know why she thinks that," June said.

Rose didn't say anything.

The girls went to their lockers. Then

they hurried to volleyball practice. They were the last to get there. They quickly got ready to practice.

"Run in place first," Coach Dale said.

The girls ran in place for about five minutes.

Coach Dale blew her whistle. Then she said, "Now time to do stretching exercises."

It helped June to run. And to do the exercises. She was no longer upset with Mrs. Frey.

Coach Dale said, "You all need to practice your serves. Be sure you get the ball over the net. Try to place the ball where you want it. And not just anywhere on the court."

June and Rose practiced their serves. Then they practiced how to pass and set and spike. And they practiced how to block.

All of the girls worked on the drills for about 20 minutes.

Then Coach Dale said, “Time to play our first game. Same teams as last time. Keep your mind on the game. And not on something else.”

The starting team played the back-up team. June and Rose were both on the starting team.

“Rose, you serve first,” Coach Dale said.

“Show them how well you can serve,” June said.

Rose served better than anyone on the team.

Rose hit an overhand serve. It was a good serve. The other team wasn’t able to hit it back. June’s team got a point.

“Way to go, Rose,” June said.

Rose hit three more good serves. And June’s team got three more points.

“Keep it up, Rose,” June said.

Then Rose hit a serve out of bounds.

"Too bad, Rose. But we got four points," June said.

Kim served next. She was on the back-up team. Her serve hit the net.

June didn't think Kim was a good player. She was glad Kim was not on the starting team.

Soon it was June's turn to serve. June got ready to serve.

Coach Dale said, "Watch where your feet are, June. And be sure to stay behind the line when you serve."

June looked down. Her feet were not on the line.

"My feet aren't on the line," June said.

Why did Coach Dale say that to her? She didn't say that to the other girls.

But sometimes June forgot to watch where her feet were. And she was standing on the line.

Chapter 3

It was the next afternoon. June was on her way to the gym. Rose was with her.

June said, "I'm glad we have a game today. And not just practice."

Rose said, "I'm glad too. A game is always more fun than practice."

June was ready to play. She was glad when the game started. They were playing Hillman High.

One team wasn't better than the other. The two teams were about the same.

Hillman won the first set. Carter High won the second.

It was the last set of the game. Hillman

was ahead. But Carter could still win. The winner would win the match.

Rose said, "We can still win. Just stay ready for the ball."

Rose said that to all of the team. Not just to June.

Kim was playing. Coach Dale had put her in to sub. Kim was on the front row. She was in front of June.

A Hillman player served the ball.

Rose yelled, "Be ready. Here it comes."

The ball was coming at June. She knew she could pass the ball to Rose. And Rose could set the ball.

The ball wasn't hit as hard as June thought it would be. She had to step up to hit the ball. Kim stepped back to hit the ball. They bumped into each other.

June almost fell. And she couldn't pass the ball to Rose. The ball hit on the court next to June.

It was a point for Hillman.

Kim quickly turned around. She said, "Are you OK, June?"

June said, "Watch what you are doing. Don't ever bump into me again. I could have passed that ball to Rose. But we lost the point."

Kim said, "Sorry. I didn't know you were going to hit the ball."

"You don't know a lot of things. Like how to play volleyball," June said.

Kim was on the back-up team. She should have been sitting on the bench. Then she would not have bumped into June.

Coach Dale sent in a sub for June.

Why should she have to leave the game? It was Kim's fault they lost the point. Not hers. So why did the coach blame her?

June went over to Coach Dale. She

said, "Why did you take me out of the game? It was not my fault. It was Kim's fault. Not my fault."

Coach Dale looked mad. She said, "Go sit on the bench. Don't get up. And don't say anything else."

June didn't know why the coach seemed mad at her. She had not done anything wrong.

June sat on the bench and watched the rest of the game. Carter High didn't play well. They didn't play like the same team. It was easy for Hillman to win the game.

The Hillman team was very excited. The Carter team was very quiet. And no one said anything to June.

June tried to talk to some of the girls. But no one would talk to her.

"Why do they seem mad at me? I didn't do anything wrong," June said to Rose.

Rose said, “We had a chance to win. But you upset the team. So we didn’t play well after that. Do you know how unkind you were to Kim? And how bad you made the team look?”

“I did not make the team look bad,” June said.

Rose said, “Yes, you did. You were yelling at your own teammate. Just think how bad that made us look.”

“Kim bumped into me,” June said.

Rose said, “Maybe it was the other way. Maybe you bumped into her.”

“Now you are taking her side. That is not fair to me,” June said.

Rose said, “And you were not fair to Kim. You are my best friend, June. But sometimes you are not very nice.”

How could Rose talk to her that way? They were best friends.

Chapter 4

June started to get ready to go home. She was upset with Kim. And Coach Dale. And now Rose. Why did everyone pick on her? It was not fair.

June got her things. She started to leave the gym. She saw Coach Dale talking to Kim.

Marge walked over to June. Marge was in one of June's classes. She was there to see the match. She didn't play on the team.

Marge said, "I saw Kim bump into you. I am glad you weren't hurt. I see her talking to Coach Dale. I hope she isn't trying to blame you."

June hoped Kim wasn't trying to blame her. But why did Marge think Kim was?

"It was her fault. So why would Kim blame me?" June said.

"I don't think she likes you," Marge said.

That surprised June.

She said, "Why? I haven't done anything to Kim."

Marge said, "I don't know why. But the other girls say she doesn't like you."

"What girls say that?" June asked.

Coach Dale called to June. She said, "Don't leave yet, June. I need to talk to you."

Why did Coach Dale want to see her? Was it to tell her it was Kim's fault? Not hers. Or had Kim really tried to put the blame on her?

June hurried over to see what Coach Dale wanted.

Coach Dale said, "I took you out of the game. And I need to make sure you know why, June."

June said, "I know why. You blame me because the ball hit the court. It was not my fault. It was Kim's fault."

"It wasn't anyone's fault. Sometimes players bump into each other on the court. They shouldn't. But they do," Coach Dale said.

That surprised June. Then why did Coach Dale take her out of the game? She had thought she knew why.

"So why did you take me out of the game?" June asked.

Coach Dale said, "Because you lost your temper. You upset the other girls. They didn't play well after that. And we lost the game."

Why should she be blamed because the other girls didn't play well?

"Maybe they played badly because I wasn't in the game. Not because I upset them," June said.

Coach Dale said, "Your sub is a good player. So that is not why. We not only lost the game. But you yelled at a teammate. I will not have that on my team."

"I almost fell down because Kim bumped into me," June said.

"But she didn't plan to do that. If you lose your temper again, you will be off the team," Coach Dale said.

"For how long?" June asked.

"The rest of the season," Coach Dale said.

"You don't mean that," June said.

Coach Dale said, "Yes, I do, June. So don't lose your temper again."

Chapter 5

It was the next day. June was on her way to lunch. She got to the lunch room before Rose did. She got her tray. Then she went over to a table and sat down.

Marge hurried in the lunch room. She quickly got her tray. She looked around the room until she saw June. She hurried over to June's table.

"OK for me to sit down?" she asked.

"Sure," June said.

Marge sat down. Then she said, "When did you and Zack break up?"

That surprised June a lot. She and Zack had not broken up.

June said, "Why did you ask me that? We haven't broken up."

"Oh. I thought you had," Marge said.

"Why did you think that?" June asked. June could tell Marge knew something she didn't. What was it?

"Zack and Kim were eating lunch together," Marge said.

June said, "How do you know? You don't eat at the same time they do."

"I heard they did," Marge said.

Marge didn't see them herself. And June knew Zack would not eat with another girl.

"You heard wrong," June said.

Marge said, "No, I didn't. Everyone is talking about it. We all thought the two of you had broken up."

Rose sat down at the table. June had not seen her come in the lunch room.

Rose said, "What are you talking about, Marge?"

Marge said, "Zack was eating lunch with Kim today. So I thought he and June had broken up."

"Well, they haven't," Rose said.

Rose and Marge looked at each other.

Then Marge said, "I see Gail. I forgot I told Gail I would eat lunch with her. See you later."

Marge got up and hurried over to Gail.

Rose said, "I can tell you are mad. But don't listen to Marge. She just told you that to upset you."

June said, "Maybe she did. But she said everyone was talking about it. Did you hear anything about it?"

At first Rose did not answer. But then she said, "Yes."

So Zack was eating lunch with Kim.

Rose said, "I'm sure Zack had a good reason for eating with Kim. So don't get mad at him. First find out why he was eating with her."

June said, "I know why. Kim is trying to take Zack away from me."

"Kim would not do that. She is not that kind of girl," Rose said.

June said, "Yes, she is. She wants my boyfriend. To get even with me. For what I said to her when she bumped into me."

"You are wrong, June," Rose said.

June got up from the table. She did not feel like eating.

June said, "I have to talk to Zack."

She knew where his next class was.

"Wait, June," Rose said.

But June did not wait.

Chapter 6

June put her food in a trash can. And then she put her tray up. She started to the lunch room door. She was in a hurry to find Zack.

Marge called to her. Marge said, "What's wrong, June? Where are you going?"

June didn't answer. She didn't want to talk to Marge.

Marge hurried over to June. She started walking next to June.

Marge said, "Where are you going? Are you going to look for Kim? That is what I would do."

June stopped. Marge was right. She should go look for Kim. And not Zack.

"Do you know where Kim is now?" June asked.

"Not right now. But I know where her next class is. She has history with me," Marge said.

"Where?" June asked.

Marge told her.

Then Marge said, "I would go with you, June. But I have to go to my locker. I'll get to the classroom as soon as I can."

But June didn't care how soon Marge got there.

June hurried down the hall to Kim's classroom. She was going to wait outside the door until Kim came. She knew Kim would be there soon.

June saw Gail.

Gail walked up to June. She said, "Are you OK, June? You look upset."

June was too mad to answer.

Then June saw Kim. She hurried over to Kim.

Kim looked surprised to see June.

June said, "Quit trying to take Zack away from me. He is my boyfriend. Not yours. Stay away from him."

The other students stopped and looked at them. But June did not care.

Kim looked even more surprised. She said, "What are you talking about? I am not trying to take Zack away from you."

"I know all about you eating lunch with Zack. And I am telling you now. Stay away from him," June said.

Kim said, "You have it all wrong. I wasn't trying to take Zack away from you. He asked me to eat lunch with him."

That made June even more upset. She said, "Don't lie to me. I know what you are trying to do. You are trying to

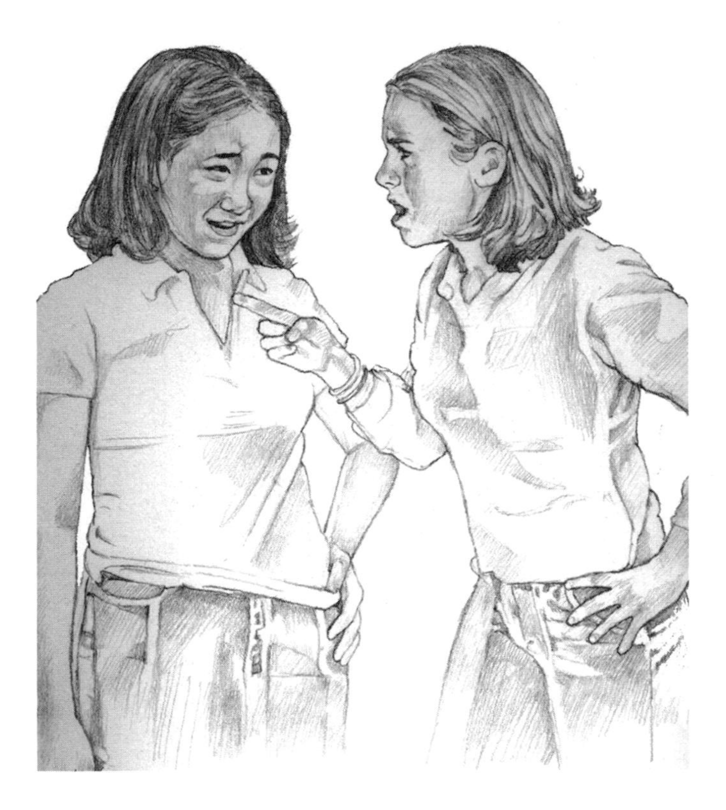

get back at me. Because I said you don't know how to play volleyball."

Kim said, "I am not after Zack. And I don't care what you said about me. Because I do know how to play volleyball."

Rose hurried up to June. She said, "I have been trying to find you, June. I thought you went to Zack's classroom. Come on. Or you will be late to class."

"I have a lot more to say," June said.

Rose said, "No, you don't. Let's go. Everyone is looking at you."

"I don't care," June said. And she didn't care.

She had more to say. And she was not going to go until she said it.

But she didn't get to say more to Kim.

Other students got between her and Kim. Kim hurried into her classroom. Some students stood in the doorway. So June could not go in there after her.

Chapter 7

June couldn't talk to Kim any more. So she went to class. She and Rose were not in the same class.

June had English. Coach Mann was her teacher. June knew she would be late. But she did not care.

And she was late.

Coach Mann looked at June. He pointed to a paper on the wall by the door. He went on with class. He didn't say anything to June about being late.

June wrote her name and the time on the paper. Then she went to her desk and sat down.

Griff sat behind her. He said, "Now you have to write a paper."

He said it so just June could hear him. And no one else.

Late students had to write a two page paper. It had to be about why they should get to class on time. So almost no one was ever late.

Griff said, "Two pages. Due tomorrow. About why you should be on time."

June wanted to tell him to leave her alone. But she didn't. She didn't want Coach Mann to see her talking.

June was too upset to keep her mind on class. She was glad when it was over.

She went to science class. Rose met her outside of their science class.

Rose said, "You still look mad. Were you late to English?"

"Yes," June said.

"What did Coach Mann say?" Rose asked.

June said, "Nothing. He just pointed to the late sign-in sheet."

"So that is why you are still mad. You have to write a paper," Rose said.

June said, "I don't care. It was worth it to tell Kim what I thought."

"So you are still mad at Kim. I was hoping you would not be," Rose said.

June said, "Why shouldn't I be? She's trying to take my boyfriend."

The warning bell rang. Rose said, "We need to go in class."

The girls went in the classroom and sat down.

Mrs. Frey looked over at June. June was sure Mrs. Frey could tell she was mad. But Mrs. Frey didn't say anything to her.

Rose said, "Stay calm, June. And don't

get upset with Mrs. Frey today. Keep quiet. And don't say anything. Unless she asks you something."

June was still too mad to keep her mind on science. How dare Kim go after her boyfriend? Was Kim just mad at her about the game? Or had she wanted to date Zack all along?

June thought the class would never end. She was glad when it did.

She hurried out of the class. Rose was with her.

Zack was waiting for her in the hall. June was glad to see him. But he looked very mad.

"See you at practice," Rose said. She quickly hurried off.

Zack said, "I heard about what you said to Kim. How could you say that to her?"

That surprised June. Why was Zack

mad at her? She had not done anything wrong.

"Kim is trying to take you away from me," June said.

Zack said, "No, she isn't."

June said, "Yes, she is. That is why she sat with you at lunch. I said she did not know how to play volleyball. And she is trying to get back at me."

"You might do something like that. But Kim would not. I asked her to sit with me. She was helping me with my science. I needed some help with my homework. And I had to turn it in right after lunch," Zack said.

June didn't believe him.

"Kim isn't in your science class," June said.

Zack said, "No, she isn't. But we have the same teacher. And my class does the same work her class does."

June didn't know what to say.

Zack said, "You know I need help on science. I told you I did. But we don't have the same teacher. So you can't help me. But Kim can."

"I'm sorry," June said.

"Don't tell me. Tell Kim," Zack said.

June wasn't going to tell Kim she was sorry.

Zack still looked mad.

He said, "No way. I am tired of you always getting mad about nothing. Find a new boyfriend."

He stomped off.

"Wait," June called after him. But Zack did not wait.

June was sure he didn't mean what he said. Or did he?

Chapter 8

June went to practice. She wanted to play volleyball. But she didn't want to see Kim.

She saw Rose in the gym.

Rose said, "What did Zack say? Why was he eating with Kim?"

"To get help on science homework. He had to turn it in right after lunch. And he and Kim have the same teacher," June said.

"I told you he would have a good reason. But you still look upset. What is wrong now?" Rose asked.

"Zack is mad at me for what I said to

Kim. He told me to find a new boyfriend," June said.

"I'm sorry, June. But don't worry. He is just mad now. He will get over it," Rose said.

"I hope so," June said. But she was not so sure he would.

Rose said, "Don't be upset today, June. And be nice to Kim. Just think about how much you like to play. And not about Zack."

Kim was on the back-up team. So June didn't have to play on the same team with her.

June stayed as far away from Kim as she could. So they didn't have to talk to each other.

June was glad when practice was over. She was in a hurry to get home. She hoped Zack would call her. So they could make plans for the weekend. But he didn't call.

June saw Zack in the hall the next day. But he didn't talk to her. And he didn't call her over the weekend.

June saw him in the hall Monday morning. She walked over to him.

She said, "We need to talk, Zack."

Zack said, "We don't have anything to talk about. I told you. Find a new boyfriend."

He walked off and left June standing there. Others were looking at her. She tried to look like she didn't care.

Rose walked up to her. They started to walk down the hall.

"What did Zack say?" Rose asked.

"That we didn't have anything to talk about. And to find a new boyfriend," June said.

"I am sorry, June. Give him time. Maybe he will change his mind," Rose said. But June wasn't sure he would. He had never been that mad at her before.

June was still on the volleyball team. And that would keep her busy for a few more weeks. She would just think about volleyball. And not about Zack.

It did not matter about Zack. Or so she told herself.

Chapter 9

The next day June saw Zack in the hall. He didn't talk to her. And she didn't try to talk to him.

After school she had a volleyball game. Carter High was playing Glen High. Glen High had a very good team.

Rose said, "We can win today. We just need to think about what we are doing."

June was playing a good game. She tried not to think about Zack. But she hoped he was there to see her play.

It was still the first game of the match. Glen High was ahead 10-8. They had been ahead most of the game.

It was Rose's turn to serve.

June said, "Put us ahead, Rose."

"Stay ready for the ball," Rose said. She said that to all of the Carter team.

Rose hit an underhand serve. It hit the court between two Glen players.

"A point for us. Keep up the good work," June yelled.

Rose's next serve was an overhand serve. It fell between the same two girls.

"We are tied," June yelled.

The Carter girls yelled loudly.

Rose's next serve was hit back. And a Carter girl hit the ball out of bounds.

It was Glen High's turn to serve.

The girl hit an underhand serve. She hit the ball too hard. It landed outside.

June's team got to serve. It was June's turn to serve.

"Show her how to serve," Rose yelled.

The score was still tied. June could

help her team take the lead. Then maybe they would win the first game.

June quickly got ready to serve. She hoped Zack was watching her play.

She didn't look to see where her feet were.

She hit an overhand serve. It looked like a good serve. She didn't think Glen High could hit it back.

The referee blew his whistle.

Why did he do that? No one had done anything wrong.

The referee said, "Fault. Glen High's turn to serve."

How could the referee say that? It was a good serve.

June ran over to the referee. She yelled, "That was a good serve."

The referee said, "Your foot was on the line."

June was sure her foot was not on the

line. Why did she get blamed for things she didn't do?

She yelled, "You are wrong. You don't know what you are talking about."

Coach Dale ran to June and the referee. She said, "Get off the court, June. And go sit on the bench."

June was very mad. She wanted to say more to the referee. But she went over to the bench. The coach stayed to talk to the referee.

Then Coach Dale walked over to June. She said, "You can stay on the bench until the match is over. Then you are off the team for good."

"You don't mean that," June said.

Coach Dale said, "Yes, I do. No one will act like that. And still be on my team."

June sat down on the bench. But she didn't watch the game.

She had lost Zack. She was sure of

that. He had gotten mad at her before. But he had never stayed mad at her that long. She knew it was over this time.

And she was off the volleyball team. All because she was quick to lose her temper. Mrs. Frey had been right. She did let her temper get the best of her. And it did hurt her when she did.

She had to stop letting her temper get the best of her. It would not be easy. But it had not been easy to learn to play volleyball well. With a lot of hard work she had learned to do that.

It might take a long time. And it would take a lot of hard work. But she would learn how to keep from losing her temper. But she might need some help to do it. Maybe Mrs. Frey could help her.

The next morning June went to see Mrs. Frey. "You were right, Mrs. Frey. I do let my temper get the best of me.

I think I need some help," June said.

She told Mrs. Frey about getting mad at Kim. And about getting mad at the volleyball game. Mrs. Frey said, "Maybe a class would help you. There is a class after school two days a week. It is about how to keep from losing your temper. Would you like to go to that?"

June didn't want to go to the class. But she knew she needed help. June said, "I will give it a try. Maybe it will help me." She sure hoped it would.